A Blue Banner Biography

Paris Hilton

Jennifer Torres

Mitchell Lane
PUBLISHERS
P.O. Box 196
Hockessin, Delaware 19707
Visit us on the web: www.mitchelllane.com
Comments? email us: mitchelllane@mitchelllane.com

Mitchell Lane PUBLISHERS

Printing 1 2 3 4 5 6 7 8 9

Blue Banner Biographies

Library of Congress Cataloging-in-Publication Data

Torres, Jennifer.
Paris Hilton / by Jennifer Torres.
p. cm. -- (A blue banner biography)
Includes bibliographical references and index.
ISBN 1-58415-382-2 (library bound)
1. Hilton, Paris, 1981– 2. Celebrities—United States—Biography—Juvenile literature. 3. Socialites—United States—Biography—Juvenile literature. 4. Models (Persons)—United States—Biography—Juvenile literature 5. Actors—United States—Biography—Juvenile literature. I. Title. II. Series.
CT275.H59926T67 2006
973. 931'092—dc22

2005012782

ABOUT THE AUTHOR: Jennifer Torres is a freelance writer and newspaper columnist based in Central Florida. Her articles have appeared in newspapers, parenting journals, and women's magazines across the country and Canada. When she's not writing she enjoys spending time at the beach with her husband John and their five children, Timothy, Emily, Isabelle, Daniel, and Jacqueline.

PHOTO CREDITS: Cover, p. 4 Jeff Vespa; p.10 Jim Smeal/WireImage; p. 14 Jamie Kondrchek ; p. 20 Peter Kramer/Getty Images; p. 23 Dave Bennett/Getty Images; p. 27 WireImage

PUBLISHER'S NOTE: The following story has been thoroughly researched, and to the best of our knowledge, represents a true story. While every possible effort has been made to ensure accuracy, the publisher will not assume liability for damages caused by inaccuracies in the data, and makes no warranty on the accuracy of the information contained herein. This story has not been authorized nor endorsed by Paris Hilton.

A Blue Banner Biography

Paris considers her teacup Chihuahua Tinkerbell part of the family. She takes the dog everywhere with her. Tinkerbell even has her own clothes, hats and shoes.

CHAPTER 1

Missing Tink

Tinkerbell is missing!

The tiny little dog was gone. Her owner, the wealthy heiress Paris Hilton, was frantic.

Usually when someone loses her dog she puts up Missing signs. Paris did post signs. She also offered a $5,000 reward for Tinkerbell's safe return.

In addition to Tinkerbell, Paris has three Pomeranians. Their names are Dolce, Sebastian, and Prince. But Tinkerbell is very special to Paris. She is a teacup Chihuahua. She is called that because her whole body can fit right inside a teacup. Paris takes Tink, as she lovingly calls her, everywhere. Usually Tink rides in a fancy dog carrier that looks like a purse. Paris takes her on planes and in restaurants. She dresses her in jackets and tiny sneakers. She also buys her scarves and jeweled collars.

Yes, Tinkerbell is one lucky pooch. She's even written a book. Well, not really, but someone wrote a book and pretended to be writing in Tinkerbell's own words.

The book is called *The Tinkerbell Hilton Diaries: My Life Tailing Paris Hilton*. In it, "Tinkerbell" talks about her first day as Paris Hilton's dog. It says: "I've been Paris Hilton's dog for just under 24 hours. I've been on both coasts, two airplanes and three parties."

Being an heiress means that Paris comes from a very rich family and will inherit a lot of money.

Paris has also revealed she lets her dog choose her boyfriends. She said if her pooch approves of a man, she would consider him a worthy suitor.

"Tink has a big say. If she likes a guy, I know they're good," said Hilton. "I'd go out with a guy who was really funny and honest, or someone Tinkerbell really liked."

Losing Tinkerbell was a major downer in Paris's life. Luckily—and quite mysteriously—Tinkerbell showed up about a week after she went missing. (It was also about a week before the Tinkerbell book was released. Could Tinkerbell's disappearance have been a publicity stunt?) No one talked about how or where Tinkerbell was found or whether anyone received the big reward. For Paris, the important thing was that Tinkerbell was home and life could return to normal.

But normal for Paris Hilton isn't necessarily what's normal for most people. Being an heiress means that Paris comes from a very rich family and will inherit a lot of money one day. She is the great-granddaughter of Conrad Hilton. He founded the Hilton hotels chain. The Hilton family is said to have a fortune of about $300 million. Paris has said, "I live a fantasy life. It's not a fantasy to me, because that's all I know, but a lot of people are interested."

For example, for her twenty-first birthday, she threw five parties for herself. They were held in New York, Las Vegas, London, Hollywood, and Tokyo. She says that for her, every day is a party—so she had to make her birthday extra special!

And speaking of Las Vegas, Paris has a hotel named after her there. It's called the Paris Hilton. She also has a chain of nightclubs called Club Paris.

In fact, Paris lives a very unique life. And despite all the media attention, the woman is still a bit of a mystery. She became famous because she is a wealthy heiress—but she has a knack for keeping herself in the spotlight. Wherever Paris goes, the newspaper writers and photographers follow. They put Paris's picture on magazine covers and write stories about her lavish lifestyle. After a while, people were asking, "Who is Paris Hilton and why is she famous?" The answer is clear. Paris has a certain something the public loves—and she isn't afraid to have fun. She's smart when it comes to creating publicity. Some things she has done haven't seemed all that bright, but she's found that even negative publicity has its value. It wasn't long before Paris had become a real celebrity.

Paris has a certain something the public loves—and she isn't afraid to have fun.

CHAPTER 2

A "Star" Is Born

Paris Whitney Hilton was born February 17, 1981, in New York, New York, to Rick and Kathy Hilton. Right from the start it was clear her life was going to be very different from most children's.

Paris's main home wasn't an apartment or a house. It was a hotel—a really big and very fancy hotel in Manhattan called the Waldorf-Astoria. It was one of the Hilton hotels. The family owned the whole building.

The Waldorf-Astoria wasn't their only home. The Hilton family also had homes in Beverly Hills, California, and in the Hamptons on Long Island, New York. They traveled back and forth between them.

Paris's parents were very well known because of the Hilton name. Hilton hotels were everywhere in the United States and across the world.

The Hilton family also had some celebrities among them.

To start with, Paris's great-grandfather, Conrad Hilton, married famous actress Zsa Zsa Gabor. Paris's grandfather,

Conrad "Nicky" Hilton Jr., was the first husband of glamorous Elizabeth Taylor.

Paris's mother, Kathy Richards, was a television star when she was a child. Kathy's sisters, Kim and Kyle Richards, have starred in films and television series. Among many other projects, they appeared in the 1975 Disney movie *Escape to Witch Mountain*. Kim was also in the movie's 2002 follow-up, *The Blair Witch Mountain Project*, and the TV series *Nanny and the Professor*. Kyle was in the series *Little House on the Prairie.*

The Hilton sisters were inseparable as young girls. They grew up surrounded by maids and butlers.

From an early age, Paris wanted fame. But she didn't want to be famous because she had a famous family. Her dreams earned her the nickname Star.

"I don't want to be known as the granddaughter of the Hiltons. I want to be known as Paris," she said.

When Paris was almost three years old, her sister, Nicky, was born.

The Hilton sisters were inseparable as young girls. They grew up surrounded by maids and butlers. Anything they wanted they usually received. They were pampered and spoiled.

The suite they lived in at the Waldorf-Astoria was on the thirtieth floor. Their parents let them order breakfast, lunch, dinner, or snacks from room service whenever they wanted to. A waiter from the hotel's restaurant would bring their prepared meal on a fancy tray right to their suite.

Even as young girls, Paris Hilton (on the left) and her sister Nicky Hilton (on the right) were a favorite focus of photographers. Their parents Kathy and Rick Hilton raised them to love the spotlight.

Paris will say, though, that the media has exaggerated many aspects of her life. She wasn't as spoiled as they've made her out to be. It is reported that Paris received $100 a week in allowance when she was thirteen. Paris says she didn't receive a credit card until she was nineteen.

Besides her sister, Nicky, Paris has two brothers, Barron and Conrad. They are much younger than their sisters.

Besides her sister, Nicky, Paris has two brothers, Barron and Conrad. They are much younger than their sisters.

Growing up, Paris was very close to another young girl. Her name was Nicole Richie. Paris thought of her as a sister, too.

Nicole was the adopted daughter of Lionel Richie, a very famous singer. When Nicole was born, her biological father couldn't take care of her. His name was Peter Michael Escovedo, and he was a member of Lionel Richie's band. Lionel Richie and his wife wanted a baby very much and gladly offered to adopt Nicole and raise her as their own child.

Paris and Nicole met at a posh day care center when they were two. Paris says her first memory of Nicole is from a school dance recital where, she recalls, "We both dressed up like little kitties."

Nicole remembers the day, too. "Everyone's doing their tap recital thing, and then you see the two of us kicking our feet and doing our own little dance," she says. "We do nothing but love each other."

After day care, Paris attended several schools. She went to the very well known and prestigious Professional

Children's School in New York City. Other students there included Christina Ricci and Macaulay Culkin.

Then she went to the Buckley School in Sherman Oaks, California. But Paris didn't stay very long.

Looking back, not continuing her education is something her friends say Paris regrets.

After that, she was sent to Connecticut, where she attended the Canterbury School. Canterbury was a boarding school, which means not only did she attend classes, but she also lived there. It was a very good school, but Paris soon became homesick. She left in her junior year.

Her parents then sent her to the Dwight School in Manhattan. They wanted Paris to have the best education. The Dwight School was certainly the place to get it. Many people had to wait for years and years to get into this school. Parents would put their children on a waiting list before they were even born.

But coming from a rich family and getting the chance to attend fancy schools doesn't guarantee you'll get the best education. Paris always had trouble in school. It was hard for her. She eventually dropped out and earned a GED instead of a regular diploma. Against her parents' wishes, she chose not to attend college.

Looking back, not continuing her education is something her friends say Paris regrets. But at the time, Paris had only one thing on her mind: fame.

CHAPTER 3

Model Behavior

Although Paris didn't stay in any one school very long, she did manage to get leading roles in two high school plays. She was chosen to play the title role in *Annie*, as well as Anne Frank in a production of *The Diary of Anne Frank*.

She loved acting, but after high school, roles were hard to find.

In 2000, she decided to give modeling a try. Why? For the fun of it!

Paris is naturally thin and tall, which made her the perfect candidate for the fashion show runway. It also helped that she loves fashion. Shopping for clothes is one of her favorite activities. Spending $8,000 in one day isn't unusual—that's $8,000 on one dress! On the other hand, she says you don't need to spend a lot to look good. When she doesn't have to dress in high fashion, she often likes to wear sweat suits—as long as they are feminine and made of cashmere or velour.

As she got older, Paris began modeling in fashion shows. Her tall and thin physique and her love for fashion made her perfect for the runway.

She also loves shoes, especially strappy high heels. She claims she can run better in high heels than in tennis shoes. But shoes are sometimes hard to find because she wears a size 11. Paris has paid top dollar to have the shoes she wanted made in her size.

Paris began to make a name for herself as a model. She appeared in shows for designers like Marc Bouwer and Catherine Malandrino.

> ***Shoes are sometimes hard to find because she wears a size 11. Paris has paid top dollar to have shoes made in her size.***

Her image also began to appear in magazine advertisements. National magazines such as *GQ*, *Vanity Fair*, and *FHM* began featuring pictures of her.

Soon people were asking, "Who's that girl?"

So many people were wondering about Paris that *People* magazine decided to run a profile of her and her sister, Nicky, who was also getting public attention.

Even though Paris was modeling, that wasn't the reason she was becoming famous. The sisters were becoming celebrities just for being young, beautiful, and rich.

The Hilton sisters enjoyed their popularity. They always had an active social life, with scores of parties and travels to faraway places at a moment's notice. But now their social life was becoming busier by the second. Everyone wanted them at their party, art show, fashion show, and club opening. Paris and Nicky loved nothing better than going out and having fun with friends at the latest nightclub or fanciest restaurant.

Everywhere they went, the paparazzi followed.

Paparazzi are the photographers who follow celebrities in order to take their picture. They can sell the pictures to magazines and newspapers. Many of them are very aggressive and will follow celebrities anywhere. Often the person being photographed gets annoyed by the paparazzi because they are so nosy and very pushy.

After about a year of modeling, Paris decided to try acting again. She was offered a small part in the movie "Zoolander."

For Paris, the attention was exactly what she wanted. She loved the interest and planned to keep people interested.

After about a year of modeling, Paris decided to try acting again. She was offered a small part in the movie *Zoolander*. The movie starred comedian Ben Stiller, who played a famous model. It was a funny take on the modeling industry, and Paris played herself in it.

In 2003 she appeared in the movie *Pauly Shore Is Dead*. It was a comedy that was released only in Australia. Once again, she played herself.

Playing "herself" over and over wasn't what Paris had in mind when she decided to be an actress. It seemed directors just wanted her in their movies because she was so recognizable.

Paris was very serious when said stated that she "has no desire to be Paris Hilton in every movie. I want to be an actress."

CHAPTER 4

The Simple Life Calls

In 1965, a humorous television show called *Green Acres* debuted. Starring Eddie Albert and Eva Gabor, it was about a lawyer and his wife, who is a socialite and an heiress. The husband had always wanted to be a farmer, so they leave their fancy home in the big city to live on a farm in a crazy small town.

In each episode the heiress has to deal with the country and everything that comes with it, like farm animals, hay, and tractors. Of course, she can't seem to figure out life on the farm, and her situation makes for a very funny show. *Green Acres* ran for seven seasons.

In 2003 Paris was offered a television show based on the idea behind *Green Acres*. The show was to be called *The Simple Life*. The difference with this show is that instead of a husband and wife, it would be about two city girls trying to live in the country. And it would be a reality show, not a scripted sitcom. Again, Paris would be playing herself, but this time she was excited about it.

Producers had wanted Nicky Hilton to star in the show with her sister. Nicky turned it down. She had no intention of spending any time in the country, and there was no changing her mind.

"She had a boyfriend at the time, and didn't want to leave," Paris explained. "She's from New York. She was not, like, into moving to a small town, so I picked Nicole, my best friend since I was two years old."

Before leaving to tape the show, the girls went on a huge shopping spree. They spent $5,000 on Rodeo Drive.

It was a deal. Paris and Nicole Richie were set to star.

Before leaving to tape the show, the girls went on a huge shopping spree. They spent $5,000 in the high-end shops that line Rodeo Drive. They bought hats, sunglasses, shoes, and a fancy carry bag for Tinkerbell.

That night their families decided to host a big party. More than 100 close friends came to wish them good luck.

But the girls were nowhere to be found.

For Paris, "an entrance is everything." At this party, a helicopter with a huge, pink banner that read "Paris & Nicole" approached the party. When it landed, Paris and Nicole emerged and greeted their friends.

After the celebration, the two friends had to turn over all their credit cards, cash, and cell phones. When asked what she would miss most, Paris admitted it would be her cell phone.

Indeed, as the world found out in February 2005, Paris kept all her personal affairs on her cell phone. Computer hackers stole her cell phone contents and posted them on the Internet. Dozens of celebrity names and addresses, personal e-mails, and photographs were made public. Some people on the list were getting a hundred phone calls an hour. Finally, with the help of the FBI, their privacy was restored.

Once the girls were on the plane to start their "simple life," the cameras started rolling.

Paris and Nicole had no idea where they were going. When the plane landed, they found themselves in Arkansas. They had to drive a pickup to what would be their home for the next thirty days. They would live there without money or luxuries. It was a farm in Altus, a small town of about 800 people.

Paris's family had their doubts. They told Paris they didn't think she could go a whole month without her credit cards and fancy surroundings.

"We're doing this to prove everyone wrong," said Paris.

The show was a hit. It was also a lot of hard work for two girls who never really had to work hard before.

The show was a hit. It was also a lot of hard work for two girls who never really had to work hard before.

"It was more than milking cows," said Paris. "We had so many jobs. We worked in fast-food restaurants, as taxidermists, in a gas station, as commercial fishermen."

In 2004, Paris and Nicole starred in *The Simple Life 2: Road Trip.* This time the girls drove across America and had adventures in different small towns.

Because of the show's popularity, in 2005 a third season followed. In *The Simple Life: Interns,* the girls took on a variety of

Paris Hilton and Nicole Richie met when they were little girls. They became best friends. The pair teamed up for the television show The Simple Life.

different jobs. They worked as flight attendants, mind readers, and matchmakers. Nicole brought her two dogs, Honey Child and Foxy Cleopatra, along for the ride.

After taping three seasons of the show, it seems Paris has proved to everyone who thought she couldn't handle hard work that they were wrong. She is not just another pretty face. She's strong and determined and willing to get her hands dirty.

In between her television shows, Paris also wrote a book called *Confessions of an Heiress: A Tongue-in-Chic Peek Behind the Pose.* In it, she gives the public a glimpse of the Paris she wants them to see—instead of simply what the media gives them. It was published in 2004.

The New York debutante was finally getting noticed for something other than her millions of dollars.

In between her television shows, Paris also wrote a book called "Confessions of an Heiress: A Tongue-in-Chic Peek Behind the Pose."

CHAPTER 5

Wanting It All

Paris was very happy that people liked her television show. She was also happy to have the chance to spend so much time with her best friend, Nicole. By early 2005, though, that friendship was apparently over. The two parted ways. While the split was made public, the reasons were not. Nicole would be replaced on the next season of *The Simple Life*; the show's next backdrop would be Hawaii.

Meanwhile, Paris still hoped to find success on the big screen, in movies. Her big dream was to be a famous movie star.

Paris did get cast in a few small roles in movies. She appeared in *Nine Lives*, *Wonderland*, *Raising Helen*, *The Hillz*, and *Pledge This!* However, they were very small parts, and none of the movies were a hit. In fact, most were bombs. Finally, in May 2005, *House of Wax* was released, and Paris had a lead part. Her costars spoke highly of her acting skills, and one reviewer commented, "She is a natural entertainer."

Paris Hilton has become a fashion icon. Everyone watches to see what she will wear next. If Paris thinks "it's hot," many designers will too.

On its opening weekend, the movie came in second in box office sales, pulling in a respectable $12.2 million.

"Getting photographed and getting treated like a star is fun. But having a dream and actually making it happen is so much more thrilling," she wrote. "Now I know I really can do anything I want."

Paris has also continued to model. She was the 2004 Guess Girl and was featured in the ad campaign for the fall 2004 clothing line.

Paris has also continued to model. She was picked to be the 2004 Guess Girl and was featured in the ad campaign for the fall 2004 clothing line.

Paris has been a frequent guest star on a variety of TV shows. Besides talk shows, she has appeared on *The O.C.*, *Las Vegas*, and *The George Lopez Show*. She has also hosted *Saturday Night Live!*

Having tried modeling and acting, Paris decided to give singing a try. She took vocal lessons for a while and then went to a studio to record some songs.

Not knowing too much about the recording industry, she asked some friends to help her. When you are rich and famous like Paris, you have some pretty rich and famous friends. One of Paris's friends was J.C. Chasez of the well-known boy band 'N Sync. J.C. and his producer, Rob Boldt, agreed to help Paris create her sound. The music is described as dance-pop: a little bit Beyoncé and a little bit Jessica Simpson.

As if modeling, acting, and singing weren't enough, Paris decided to design her own line of jewelry. It is called the Paris Hilton Collection, and it's made of sterling silver and crystals. It is also not too expensive. Most pieces cost between $18 and $60. The jewelry line has become very popular. She has also designed fragrances and a line of makeup.

Setting aside time to help those in need is also important to Paris. She donates her time to many charities, including Toys for Tots, a group that provides gifts to needy children during the holidays. She signed a stapler for the Staples Foundation for Learning in the Staples "Staplers to the Stars" online charity auction. The stapler brought in more than $4,100.

Setting aside time to help those in need is also important to Paris. She donates her time to many charities, including Toys for Tots.

Paris also helps to organize charity events. One is a casino night to benefit New York's Room to Grow charity. She has even hosted a charity auction in her own home.

One of her favorite charities is Paradise Kids, an Australian organization that cares for seriously ill children. Paris says she enjoys her time with these kids more than any time she could spend at the fanciest party or ritziest event. According to News.com, "Paris was so moved by the plight of these youngsters that she vowed to host a charity concert in Los Angeles to honor them."

"I just feel I have the time and the resources to help out," said Paris. "They're just so sweet. I love children."

By spring of 2005, Paris was ready to get serious as a businessperson. "I'm glad I got the partying out of my system when I was young, because now I'm so over it and I can focus on my career," she said. "Now I'm trying to build an empire. I don't want to be known as this Hilton hotel girl my whole life. I want to make my own name."

The public exposure she's built up over the past few years may have been a business move in itself.

Still, she relies on her father, Rick Hilton, for sound business advice. "Never settle," she said is the most important thing he's ever told her. "You can always get a lot more."

People have been surprised at Paris Hilton's success. Many think she is not smart enough to survive in the business world. But as Fred Khalilian, the businessman behind the line of Club Paris nightclubs, said of her, "Every day they say her fifteen minutes is up, and every day you have to add another fifteen minutes."

In fact, the public exposure she's built up over the past few years may have been a business move in itself. Where she used to go to parties just for fun, she now charges an appearance fee of $200,000 for twenty minutes. She has understandably been called a "self-promoting dynamo."

Meanwhile, Paris has been developing hobbies that aren't related to shopping. She likes to cook, bake, and bathe (using plenty of girlie products). She's also looking ahead to

Paris has always maintained a close relationship with her parents, Kathy and Rick Hilton. Her mother Kathy recently began work on her own television show So you want to be a Hilton?

marriage and starting a family. In fact, Paris recently became engaged to another *Paris*; his name is Paris Latsis, and he's the nephew of a rich Greek shipping tycoon.

Latsis, 27, proposed to Hilton, 24, after she returned from Europe to promote her horror flick *House of Wax*. The couple actually met as children but lost touch over the years. They celebrated their engagement with a big barbeque with family and friends.

With Paris following her own plans and dreams, it seems this simple girl may be more savvy than she appears.

In her book, Paris admits that anybody can be an heiress. Success doesn't depend on how much money you have. It's all in your attitude.

"I always took matters into my own hands. I wanted to be a model, actress and singer from a young age, so I told my parents and they could tell I was serious," she wrote. "In so many ways being an heiress is really all in your head. If you follow your own plans and dreams and you don't let anyone talk you out of them, then you'll start to get the hang of being an heiress."

With Paris following her own plans and dreams, it seems this simple girl may be more savvy than she appears. Then again, maybe she isn't. The mystery will keep people watching her for many years to come.

CHRONOLOGY

1981 Paris Whitney Hilton is born on February 17 in New York City.

1983 Her sister, Nicky Hilton, is born on October 5; Paris meets her future "best friend," Nicole Richie.

2000 Paris begins to make a name for herself as a model.

2001 She appears in the Ben Stiller movie *Zoolander.*

2002 Paris and Nicky begin to appear on more and more magazine covers as the "Hilton sisters" achieve celebrity status.

2003 *The Simple Life* debuts on television.

2004 Paris is selected as the new Guess Girl. *The Simple Life 2: Road Trip* debuts. Her famous saying, "That's hot," is chosen as the best catch phrase and wins a trophy at the VH1 Big in '04 Awards. Her book, *Confessions of an Heiress: A Tongue-in-Chic Peek Behind the Pose,* is published.

2005 *The Simple Life: Interns* airs. Paris and Nicole part ways. Paris appears in the *House of Wax*. She is engaged to Paris Latsis and vows to settle down and become a serious businesswoman.

FOR FURTHER READING

Books

Hilton, Paris, with Merle Ginsberg. *Confessions of an Heiress: A Tongue-in-Chic Peek Behind the Pose.* New York: Fireside, 2004.

Resin, D. *The Tinkerbell Hilton Diaries: My Life Tailing Paris Hilton.* New York: Warner Books, 2004.

Articles

Dehnart, Andy. "Nicky Hilton Said No to the Simple Life Which Will Now Air in October." *Realty Blurred, the Reality TV News Digest,* July 22, 2003.

Freydkin, Donna. "Checking In with Paris Hilton." *USA Today,* December 1, 2003.

Keck, William. "Simple Friends for Life." *USA Today TV,* June 15, 2004.

Ogunnaike, Lola. "Paris Inc." *The New York Times,* May 2, 2005.

Villarreal, Phil, "'Wax' Dispenses Terror Drip by Drip," *Arizona Daily Star,* May 5, 2005.

On the Internet

About, Primetime TV, "The Simple Life Episode Guide"

http://primetimetv.about.com/library/blsimplelife1recap1.htm

AskMen.com, "Paris Hilton, Model of the Week,"

http://www.askmen.com/women/models_150/171_paris_hilton.html

"Paris Hilton: Paris Loses Her Tinkerbell."

http://www.femalefirst.co.uk/celebrity/5562004.htm

The Internet Movie Database

http://www.imdb.com/name/nm0385296/

SELECTED TELEVISION AND MOVIE CREDITS

Movies

2006 *Bottom's Up*
2005 *Pledge This!* (also executive producer)
House of Wax
2004 *The Hillz*
Raising Helen
2003 *The Cat in the Hat*
Wonderland
L.A. Knights
2002 *QIK2JDG*
Nine Lives
2000 *Sweetie Pie*
1991 *Wishman*

Appearing as Herself

2005 *The Simple Life: Interns*
2004 *VH1 Big in '04*
Bullrun: Cops, Cars & Superstars
The Simple Life 2: Road Trip
MTV Movie Awards 2004 Pre-Show (Co-host)
2003 *The Simple Life*
Pauly Shore Is Dead
2001 *Zoolander*

Notable TV Guest Appearances

2005 *American Dreams* playing "Barbara Eden" in episode: "California Dreamin'"
Saturday Night Live playing "Host"
2004 *Veronica Mars* playing "Caitlin Ford" in episode: "Credit Where Credit's Due"
Fashion in Focus playing "Herself" in episode: "New Kids on the Block: Part 2"
The O.C. playing "Kate" in episode: "The L.A."
George Lopez playing "Ashley" in episode: "Jason Tutors Max"
Las Vegas playing "Madison" in episode: "Things That Go Jump in the Night"
2003 *Tinseltown TV* playing "Herself"

INDEX